名流詩叢
33

兩弦
Two Strings

——漢英雙語詩集

距離不一定
是隔離
有詩相繫
瞬間天涯就在隔壁
詩的精靈
還可鑽入深心裡
把苦悶化成莫大喜悅
一如長相左右
毫無距離

〔德國〕艾薇拉・辜柔維琪 (Elvira Kujovic) 著

李魁賢 (Lee Kuei-shien) ◎著／譯

Doch alles, was uns anrührt, dich und mich,
nimmt uns zusammen wie ein Bogenstrich,
der aus zwei Saiten *eine* Stimme zieht

——aus "Liebes-Lied" vom Rainer Maria Rilke

Yet everything that touches us, me and you,
takes us together like a violin's bow,
which draws *one* voice out of two separate strings.

——from "Love Poem" by Rainer Maria Rilke

可是所有觸及你我的萬物，
使我們結合猶如一道琴弓，
從兩條弦上拉出一個音響。

——摘自里爾克詩〈戀曲〉

合著者艾薇拉‧葦柔維琪與李魁賢參加2018淡水福爾摩莎國際詩歌節，於9月24日在淡水富貴角海岸燈塔前合照。

目次

第一弦・漢語篇

李魁賢　譯

老風友

老風友呀
正在期望愛情
你能找到嗎，
在如此不忠不安穩時。
你來，摸我，又走啦，
因為你只知道什麼是真愛。
只要一瞬間，只要一擁抱，
只要一擠壓和嘆息，
只是夢，一再夢想
始終不一樣，
只要多一個願望。
風友呀，為何我從來不知
你何時會來
為何總是敲我的門，
使我心戰慄，
像樺樹在等待
你來摸手臂，
吻頭髮

瞬間冷靜下來
迷失其中，
你是我的老風友，
再一次摸摸我的心
要對我忠實
在你擁抱我時，
不要想別的，
別讓你的念頭飛走
我的老情人，
停在我髮內，
在那裡安靜睡吧，
讓全世界叫喊等待
可愛老風友，請與我同在。
就像這樣愛我，你心知。
我的浪人，每朵花
都來誘惑又離棄，
每株樺樹在瘋狂引導，
我的情人，

我的風友今夜在何處
你在平靜尋找哪一根草,
你在期望哪個太陽
此時你向我款款而來
那些美麗樹枝
等待到黎明
等你親吻。
我的風友,你在哪裡?
我的風友,你在哪裡?

我的愛

寫封信給我吧
說說關於你的愛情
和你真實的愛。
你有過
多少女人？
你還能記住每個人嗎？
用一張紙，算一算，
告訴我關於每個人的
一則情史，
或者你對每位所喜愛女人
一些很特別故事。
隨你喜歡叫出她們
當然你會隱匿一些名字。
告訴我關於你的生活
和你未實現的願望。
我想知道有關你的一切。
我非常愛你，這就是
我想瞭解你全部的原因。

讓我分享你的一生。
我想在你的每一則故事中
佔有一個位置
我想成為你愛過的
每一位女人。
不要忘記這位那位
要活在她們每一位當中
再跟我一次，
再跟我一次，
再跟我一次。

新晨

無精打采凝視著某事，
我甚至無法指出
此時此刻身在何處。
沉默覺醒，
做什麼事都無聲
我頭腦裡仍然雜音
亂成一片混沌，
我無法辨識
那是什麼
而我是什麼，
我在現實還是夢裡，
不知道今日何日，
明天又是什麼
為什麼沒有人知道
為什麼新晨照舊蒞臨。

你是我的詩

親愛的，我與你同在。
我成為你的影子
也是你的太陽。
我成為你的感情
也是你的血液。
我成為你的苦戀
而你是我的詩。
你成為我的聲音
我的想像
也是我的女性夢，
我願望
成為你手中的筆，
日日夜夜，
成為你口中的草莓，
你唇間的蜜，
你未完成的夢想，
你的感動，你永恆的生命。
我正是你的、是你的、是你的
我的情人⋯⋯情人⋯⋯情人。

心愛的

只有我知道
你完美閉口守住祕密。
你眼中書寫的文字
愛人呀，只有我能明白⋯⋯

你的愛情力量
像海浪一般
再三回衝使我迷惘，
耐心等待。
我正在等候你。

你魔術手法，
把我變得思慕，
成為螢火蟲，
只有在你缺席的黑暗中
閃閃發亮
盼望更多的痛苦
我知道，只屬於我。

我是你永恆的壁爐
你一而再回來，
又一次證明你的男性魅力
計算我的每次嘆息
重新安撫我，
無怨無悔愛上我。

心愛的，我正在等候你，
因為我們無畏風和水
生與死，
我們是灰塵和灰燼
我們是火
我們是生命

愛情

讓我們愛情永遠不熄，
活生生存在，
甚至當全宇宙
已經消失
讓愛情成為光
可以引導
一切
跟著我們存在。
讓我們心中溫暖
傳遍遙遠宇宙
創造全新的世界
跟隨我們來臨。

派烏鴉過來吧

蝴蝶不飛了
我在等待一杯毒藥。
獨守我的詩句
盼望你的烏鴉飛來
已有多時。
我寫過許多信
甚至一大堆。
如果你能再來信
那就太好啦。
你不寫，天黑時，
只有你的文字是我的光。
心愛的，你住哪裡？
我還是要知道
你愛誰
派烏鴉過來吧
把你的文字送過來吧
我不想再為你相思綿綿。

閃電

你眼神閃電
或是你心靈細語
可能為這種愛內疚；
愛棲息在我乳房之間
在此植根。
在我生命裡點火
我看到
你的心如何顫動
想要隱藏
我給予的愛，
但徒然，
我們保持氣氛
在我們胸膛諦聽
心靈如何
以相同節奏呼吸，
感動自己
從那時刻起，
彼此形影不離。

雪花

若是你牽我的手，
我會興奮，
像夜來香花開
當月光
笑著敞開胸部
讓蜜蜂叮
任其吸血。
因你觸摸而暈眩
我會為你裸心，
像荷葉
我會讓渴望的雨水
滾下我的皮膚
然後
再度想念你。
你來時
我會再振奮，
我失明的眼睛會在你的虹膜復原
而我的心靈就在你心靈裡。
牽我的手吧，

把我帶進你的愛裡，
在此地我眼睛可以重見。
你不在時
我收集流下的眼淚，
在湖底
已變成鑽石。
已然成為太陽。
我們的湖在呼喚
去游泳、去沉溺。
牽我的手吧，
你知道，
愛情總是飢餓，
我們去吃吧，
到滿足為止。
愛總是會驚慌、顫慄
我已經變成雪花，
飄落在你額頭融化。
請擁我入懷
給我溫暖、溫暖、溫暖。

俘虜

我只想告訴你
我整天想念你。
我一心想在
你的土地
說你的語言
就像那裡的鳥。
鳥也已經學會用
你的語言叫我的情人
用你的鄉音說出我的心聲。
鳥在夢寐
你周邊的世界
呼吸你吐納的空氣
卻生活在我的世界。
你想像得到嗎？
我的肌膚感受到
現在你那邊正在下的雨絲
聞到在你的窗口
成長的花卉

吸到你腳下的灰塵
用我的眼睛
看到在你身旁走過
顯出嫉妒的每一張臉。
我的眼睛變成你的
你的變成我的。
你能想像到
你這男人擁有兩個心靈
我的和你的
你家在我心中
我藏你，沒有人
能在那裡找到你。
你可想像得到
我的情人呀，你是在
我的愛情俘虜營裡。

在我口袋裡

我帶著你
跟我到處去
你知道你在哪裡嗎？
在我的口袋裡。
這就是
我喜歡把手放在
口袋裡的原因，
因為我感覺到你的吻
和你的感情
在我冷得
瑟瑟發抖時
給我溫暖
當世界正在消失時
我沒有什麼遺憾……

影子

白天每個人醒來時
不好意思期待
人生的美妙驚喜。
我以誕生自你虹膜黑暗的
白影出現在你面前
我彷彿是戀愛中的女人
亦步亦趨跟隨你腳步。
我的白影靜靜環繞著你
親吻你的頸項
讓你哆嗦
讓你醒來
然後消失無蹤
很快又回到你眼裡
除了你沒有別人能夠看到
我的愛人呀！

老路

你每天
一步一步
繼續
走你的路
你一再遇到愛
像路上的絆腳石。
你已經腳痛
膝蓋流血
但無論如何
我們人生
值得的
唯一美事是
再三去愛
所以我依然躺下
像一塊新石頭
在你的老路上
親吻你流血的膝蓋
只要你繼續走
在你的路上。

雲

你漂浮在雲間
那是我送給你的
你用我的心去感受
那是神賜給我的
你用我的身體去感覺
那是你想要的
你用我的手指觸摸東西
那是你在親吻的
你用我的嘴唇飲酒
嘴唇卻把你飲盡
一滴不剩。

今晚不要來

今晚不要來
留在籠罩你的霧中
把你隱藏，從我身邊把你偷走。
你那裡，有鳥嗎？
親愛的，有樹葉嗎？
讓鳥啁啾，替我跟你說話
讓樹葉代替我的手指
撫摸擁抱你。
讓小鹿的眼睛
在我眼中想念你
把你刺痛。
今晚不要來
走出你的陰暗和昏沉
讓我成為你的太陽
讓我再度給你生命。
你知道你離開時使我多麼傷心
因為你始終沒答應我要回來。
我吻過你多少次？

我失去你多少次？
我對你說過多少次
再見讓你走？
在唯你所知的生命中
你甚至不想與我分享。
今晚不要來
因為樹葉會窸窣響
呼叫你的名字。
雲喜歡去探望你
而月亮喜歡照亮你來時路。
就留在你那裡吧
因為心痛，而我在等你
會感覺更好，像做夢。
更好，像人生
就離開久一點吧。

薩福詩簡

我忍受不住
我們二者之間的
此時情況。
到底是誰對誰
關門啦？
還是兩邊仍然開啟？
只是我們不敢走進去。
我的門向你敞開。

信件

親愛的情人，
由於人生戲弄
使我太晚遇到你。
我在夜裡摸黑自述
但願在你心中找到位置。
就像我在夜裡靜靜
為自己寫下許多詩一樣
像竊賊偷偷摸摸。
我逃離自己
尋找去投靠你的方式。
我是小小微不足道的信件。
我想討你歡心。
但我想
我如此渺小、如此空虛
誰會愛我
我如此貧乏，無可付出。
無大感情、無痛、無苦
無愛，甚至無欣羨。

我只是願望！
也許無法實現。
也許我只是絆腳石。
不然，
只要你不斷閱讀我
則我的巧慧會有成果
獲得廁身寫在你心中最後一頁
龐大優美詩篇之旁。
我是渺小微不足道的信件。

兩位先知

我的甜心呀
你的光亮啦，
你的光跟著你
不管往哪個方向
你的心逃去呼喚，
跟隨你擁抱你。
愛人呀，我倆不是愛的先知嗎？
難道我們不是永遠流浪者
總是在路上交錯。
看看右邊，我在那裡，
看看左邊，
我是你的影子在和你嬉戲，
我的摯愛，我是光
會使你目眩
所以你只能用心看我。
情人呀，你的光在這裡，
來自永恆
此後和你一起走，

永遠不會孤單，
我的甜心呀。

距離

我的思念
是你的組成份之一。
你永遠存在我的生命裡。
我們彼此相思
是愛永無止境的迴響
因此，什麼都不要問我。
只要傾聽我們之間
距離的苦悶吧。
因此，什麼都不要問我。

蝴蝶低聲

春天正在我心中盛開
每年一而再，
更加繁榮。
春天在不忠實的雲間
雲來來往往
一出生
就有飛馳的本事。
我知道，有時會帶給你
我最喜歡的丁香氣味，
瞬間就喚醒
你急切想念我。
跟你玩捉迷藏喔，
情人呀，
還有蝴蝶也以低聲翅翼
喚醒你沉睡的心
把我種植在你的花上，
情人呀，讓我永遠與你同在。

最後的詩

今天我只有再
給你寫一首詩，
像過去大聲叫喊，
只留下一個想法
我知道此後
會好想死去。
今天是我們最後日子。
這是長久以來
為你寫的最後一首詩，
對我來說
活得更長久更豐富
你和我的憶念，
但只有今天
我會再寫
然後
我會放你走，
我會吐納你，
像最後一口氣。

失去你我會
孤單了無氣息。

話語

話語
從心裡衝出來要送給你，
靜靜在你門口等待。
然而不容許敲門。
只希望
你會想聽聽怎麼說。
願和你待在家裡
一生在你胸前呼吸
與你共守在窩裡。
站在門口久久不動
仍然沒有回應。
即使站在那裡至今，
脫衣全裸
呈現你想要的全部美。

永遠

別擔心
在你遇到我時
我會不會喜歡你。
我就是愛你這個樣子。
在我看來你最美。
別擔心
如何擁抱我。
你的擁抱最美，
會使我在擁抱中迷失。
別擔心
會持續多久。
會永遠。

我不是你的薩福

你並不愛我
沒有愛過
我不是你的影子
我不存在
不在這裡也不在其他地方
我只是想
時時活下去
不值得生
不值得死
我只是感覺
要尋找一顆心
活在裡面。

The First String · 英語篇

艾薇拉·辜柔維琪　著

Old Wind

My old wind

which is looking for the love

can you find it ever

when you're so unfaithful and unstable.

You came, caressed me and go again

because you only know what is real love.

Just one moment, just one hug,

just one squeeze and a sigh

only a dream, dreamed again

and always different

just one wish more.

My wind why I never know

when you will come

and why you always knock at my door

while my heart trembles

like a birch and awaits

you to caress it's arms

it's hairs to kiss

and for a moment calm in it

that you get lost in it.

You my old wind

caress my heart one more time

and be faithful to me

while you're hugging me

do not go to another

let not your thought fly.

My experienced lovers

stay in my hair

and sleep peacefully there

let the whole world cry and waits

stay with me, my loving old wind.

Love me just so, as you only know.

My wanderer which every flower

has seduced and left

every birch in madness led

my lover

my wind where are you tonight
in which grass you seek in peace,
which sun are you looking for
while you stream to me
and whose beautiful branches
want you to kiss
waiting to the dawn.
My wind, where are you?
My wind, where are you?

My Love

Write me a letter

about your love affairs

and about your real loves.

How many women

have you had until yet ?

Can you still remember everyone?

Count them all up, on a sheet of paper

and tell me an anecdote

about each of them

or something very special

what you on each woman liked.

Call them like you want

for sure you wish some names to hide.

Tell me about your life

and your unfulfilled wishes.

I love you very much and that is why,

I want to know, about you all.

Share your whole life with me.

I wish to take a place
in your every story
and I want to be each of the women,
whom you ever loved.
Do not forget one or the other,
and live in each one of them
one more time with me,
one more time with me,
one more time with me.

New Morning

Lost meaning and lazy stare at something,
I can't even figure out
where I am at this moment.
Silence woke up
and did everything speechless
but still in my head is chaos
of the mixed sounds,
I can't recognize them
what they are
and what am I
Am I a reality or a dream,
I wonder which day is today
and what is tomorrow
and why no one knows
why the new morning still comes.

You are My Poetry

Dear Love...I am with you.
I become your shadow
and your sun.
I become your feeling
and your blood.
I become your passion
and you my poetry.
You become my voice,
my imagination
and my woman's dream,
my wish
to be a pen in your fingers,
day and night,
to be strawberry in your mouth,
honey on your lips,
your unfulfilled dream,
your touch, your eternity life.
I become just yours, just yours, just yours
my love...my love...my love.

Darling

Only I know the secret
closed behind your perfect lips.
Words written in your eyes
only I can understand my love...

On the power of your love
which like the ocean waves
comes back again and again to beguile me,
I wait patiently.
I'm waiting for you.

The magic of your Hands,
to turn me into yearning,
into a firefly,
that shines only
in the darkness of your absence
and craves for even more pain
belongs only to me, I know.

I'm your eternal fireplace
to which you return again and again,
to prove your male power once more time
and to count each of my sighs
anew and to tame me,
without grieving to love me.

I'm waiting for you my darling,
because we defy the wind and water
life and death,
we are dust and ashes
we are the fire
we are the life.

Love

Let our love never die

let it live

even when all universes

have disappeared.

Let it alone be the light

and let it be the guide

for everything

that will once exist after us.

Let the warmth of our hearts

spread through the distant universes

and let it creates all new worlds

which after us comes.

Send me a Raven

The butterflies are not flying

a cup of poison is for me waiting.

Lonely I have only my lines

It's been a while

that I saw your raven fly.

I have written many letters

even a crowd.

But if your letter came again

that would be so nice.

It is dark, you don't write

and only your words were my light.

Darling where do you live

and who do you love

I still have to know

send me a raven

send me your words

I don't want to miss you anymore.

Lightning

Lightning of your eye
or your soul's whisper
is maybe guilty for this love;
which nested between my breasts
and let the roots.
It lit a fire in my being
and I saw
how your heart trembled
and wanted to hide
It's love from me
but in vain
while we kept the air
in our chest to hear
how our souls
are in the same rhythm breathing,
they touched themselves
and from that Moment
they can't one without another.

Snowflake

If you take me by the hand
I will flourish
as the night flower blooms
when the light of the moon
laughs at it opening its breast
for the bee sting
and let its blood suckle.
Dazed by your touch
I will bare my heart for you
and like a lotus leaf
I will let the rain of longing
to roll off of my skin
and then
to miss you again.
I will rise again
when you come
my lost eyes I will recover in your iris
and my soul in yours.
Take me by the hand

lead me into your love
to this place where I can see again.
Collect my tears that have flew
in your absence
they have become diamonds
at the bottom of the lake.
They have become the Suns.
Our lake is calling us
to swim in it, to drown in it.
Take me by the hand
you know
the love is always hungry

Let us be satisfied.
Love freezes always and trembles
and I have become a snowflake
which on your brow falls and melts.
Take me in your arms
Warm me, warm me, warm me.

Prisoner

I only want to tell you

that I miss you all day.

My heart wants to be

in your land

and talk your language

as the birds there do.

It speaks already

your language my love

and my soul your dialect too.

It dreams about the world

which is around you

breaths the air which you exhale

but it lives in my world.

Can you imagine that?

My skin feels the rain

which is raining there now

smells the flower

which at your window grows

breaths the dust under your feet
and sees every face
which passed by you with jealous
with my eyes.
My eyes become yours
and you become mine.
Can you imagine that
you are the man
with two souls, mine and yours
and your home is in my mind.
I hid you there, and nobody
can you there find.
Can you imagine
you are in a prison
of my love, my love.

In my Pocket

I carry you

with me everywhere

and do you know where you are?

In my pocket.

That's why

I like it so much

to put my hands in it

because I feel your kisses

and your feelings

that warm me

when it shivers

and when cold is

when the world is going lost

I have nothing to regret.

The Shadow

Daytime when everyone wakes up

And shy expects

A nice surprise of life

I appear in front of you as a white shadow

Born in the dark of your iris

I appear like the loving woman

Which follows you on the step.

My white shadow surrounds you quietly

Kisses you on your neck

Lets you tremble

Lets you wake up

Then it disappears

Quickly again in your eye back

That nobody but you is able to see it

My love

Old Ways

Step by step you go on, on your way

every day you meet the love

again and again

like stumbling rocks on it.

You already have sore

and bloody knees.

But whatever?

The only beauty that's

worthwhile

in our life

is to love again and again

so I'm still lying down like

a new stone

on your old way

and I am kissing your bloody knees

as long as you go on

on your way.

The Cloud

You are floating in a cloud
that I have sent to you
you feel with my heart
that God gave me
You feel with my body
which you desire
You touch the things with my fingers
which you are kissing
You are drinking with my lips
and they drink you
until the last drop.

Don't Come Tonight

Don't come tonight,

stay in that fog which is swallowing you

which is hiding you and steals you from me.

Are there birds, where you are?

Are there leaves, darling?

Let those birds chirp

let it be my talk for you

and the leaves be my fingers

which caress you.

Let the deer's eye

remember you at mine

and stab you into pain.

Don't come tonight,

out of your darkness and dusk

to let me be your sun

to let me give you life again.

Do you know that your leaving hurt too much

because you never promised me to come back.

How many times have I kissed you?

How many times have I lost you?

How many times have I been saying

adieu to you and let you go

In the life only known to you

you don't want to share it even with me.

Don't come tonight

because the leaves want to rustle

and call your name.

Clouds like to look for you

and the moon likes to light you the way to me.

Stay where you are

because the pain, while I am waiting for you

nicer is, as the dream, nicer as the life

stay still a little longer away.

From Sappho

This situation
between us both
I cannot stand.
Who has now closed
the door to whom?
Or are both still open?
And we are afraid to enter.
My door is open for you.

The Letter

Dear lover,
because my life plays tricks on me
I reach you a little later.
I write myself in the dark at night
and hope I find a place in your heart.
Like one of many which I wrote
in silence for myself at night
I sneaked like a little thief.
I ran away from me
and sought my way to you.
Me the little, insignificant letter.
And I wanted to please you.
But I thought
I'am so small, so empty
who can love me
I'm so poor, I have nothing to offer.
No big feelings, no pain, no suffering,
no love, not even envy.

I am only a wish!

Maybe I will be unfulfilled.

Maybe I'm just a stumbling block.

But if not and if you keep reading me

then my cunning carried the fruits

and I'm allowed to be next to the big and beautiful ones

written on the last page of your heart.

Me, the small and insignificant letter.

Two Prophets

My sweetheart
your light turns on,
your light follows you
no matter in which direction
your heart escapes to cry,
it follows you to hug you.
Are we two not the prophets of love, my love
are we not eternal wanderers
who always cross the path of one another.
Look to the right there I am,
look to the left,
I'm your shadow who plays with you,
Dearest I am the light
that blinds your eyes
so that you can see me only with your heart.
My darling your light is here,
it comes from eternity
and goes with you afterwards,

you are never alone,
my sweetheart.

Distance

My thoughts
are one of your components.
You are forever present in my being.
Our desire for each other
Is a never-ending echo of love
Hence, ask me nothing.
Just listen the agony of the distance
Which is between us.
Hence, ask me nothing.

The Butterfly Whisper

The spring is flourishing in my heart
every year again and again,
and always nicer.
It is in unfaithful clouds
which come and go
when they want born
and get their features to be fleeting.
I know, sometimes it brings you
the smell of my favorite lilac,
just for a moment to awake
your longing and memories of me.
It plays hide-and-seek with you,
my love,
as well as the butterflies with their whispering wings do
to wake up your sleeping heart
and plant me on your flower,
so I can always be with you, my love.

The Last Poem

Only one poem more
I write for you today,
just one scream in the past,
only one left thought
and I know that afterwards
my yearning dies.
Today is our last day.
It was the last one for you
a long time ago,
for me
lived much longer and more,
the memory of you and me,
but today only
I will write again
and then
I will let you go,
I will exhale you,
like a last breath.

I will be breathless
without you alone.

The words

The words
out of the heart yanked up to send it to you,
have remained silent waiting at your door.
They were not even allowed to knock.
Nothing but the hope
you wanted to listen what about they spoke.
They would like to be by you at home
to breathe in the life on your chest
and live with you in your nest.
They stood still and long time there
and found no answer.
Even now they are standing there,
undressed and completely naked
all their beauty to show you wanted.

In Aeternum

Don't worry

when you meet me

would I like you or not.

I love you the way you are.

You're the most beautiful to me.

Don't worry

will you know how to hug me.

Your hugs are the most beautiful,

I will lose myself in them.

Don't worry

how long will it last.

It will be eternally.

I am not your Sappho

You don't love me
You never did
I am not your shadow
I do not exist
Not here and not elsewhere
I'm just a thought
from time to time lives
Not worthy of life
And not for death
I'm just a feeling

第二弦・漢語篇

李魁賢 譯

新金枝

新金枝呀
我已習慣自由
到處流浪
不論山邊海角
來無影去無蹤
喜歡與樹木嬉戲
撫摸茂密翠綠的頭髮
金髮女郎更吸引我
無論在晨曦或晚霞照耀下
呈現金枝的傳說
好像讓我看到
前生或是來世風光
我不沉湎於夢想
金枝在廣大天空下
是一道通向另一世界的橋
連接兩岸開放空間
沒有門
我從此岸走過去

不需敲門
妳就在對岸接納我
新金枝呀
妳不用揮手
或做任何信號
我在遠方就已看到妳
像陽光不需引導
沒有任何樹蔭阻擋
我只要俯身下來
就會有妳反射
像一道虹橋讓我跨越
暢流的河
我知道妳的樹枝
渴望我的光親吻
妳細緻溫柔的肌膚
我愛聽妳颯颯的歌聲
對四季的讚頌
妳是我的薩福我的繆思

我常常化身為風
習慣到處自由流浪
我的新金枝呀
無論妳在山岡或是海濱
只要妳在哪裡
我都會圍繞妳身邊
即使無影無形
妳知道，我在妳心裡！
妳知道，我在妳心裡！

心愛的

妳要我寫信給妳
說說關於我的愛情。
其實許多往事
已不復記憶。
隨時間變遷
有些事愈來愈模糊
也有些事愈來愈清晰。
我的腦筋
現在是一張白紙
此時此刻
只有妳
在我心中。
我試著寫下
聯繫過的
全部女性名字,
看起來名字剛好
都和妳一樣,
原來就是妳。

我要開始在白紙上
寫下新情史的第一頁
以妳為故事女主角
永遠記住妳，
讓妳始終活在
愛的世界裡。
這一次就是妳
這一次就是妳
這一次就是妳。

早安

早安！
妳似乎心不安。
經歷過黑暗的世界
體驗過世界的黑暗
妳聽過人民在暗中哭泣
妳看過人民在夜裡掙扎
即使新晨來臨
妳還是在關心
天空中有大鷹掠食小鳥
草原上有虎豹獅
獵殺馴鹿和綿羊
另一半的地球
陷入沒有陽光的境遇
這些確實使妳心不安
如果我在妳身旁會好些嗎？

詩是愛

神創造愛
彌漫宇宙間
神再創造詩人
歌頌愛
為日出為日落
為花香為鳥語
為小草為大樹
為猛獸為家畜
為風為雨
為快樂為悲傷

螢火蟲

生命中總有火種
永遠不息
自然會引起風動
越洋傳送薩福詩篇

聲調優美柔情
宛如天使福音
我不需等待
只要敞開心胸
共鳴滿懷

詩人宿命
就是螢火蟲
在野地黑暗中
給世界一點點
微弱的光
有人嫌太暗淡
有人獲得安慰

那幽光或許
沒有火爐溫暖
卻是心靈的希望
像獨立海邊的燈塔
指示船隻
可以安全靠岸

薩福呀
如果有一天
妳變成一隻海鷗
這裡有妳佇足的礁岩
妳可以築巢的陸地
在這裡傳衍生命

神聖的愛

愛是神聖的話語
成為福音
集真善美於一體
自太初起源
就是一切的根本
人因愛而生
人因愛而死
愛是世界的原動力
永遠神聖
永遠有溫暖
宇宙因此
生生不息

烏鴉不再飛

我想妳的時候

就寫詩

不想寫信

我會找白鴿傳送

不勞煩大烏鴉

怕那一身不祥的燕尾服

引起妳驚訝

擔心那敲門聲會使妳害怕

我知道妳不是雷諾娥

現今天空無戰事

烏鴉不再飛

我的白鴿

可以自由飛翔

天亮時

帶給妳台灣自由的消息

我會永遠記得

妳是金髮艾薇拉

暴風雨

突如其來的閃電
警報將會有
不可預料的暴風雨
天空也會受傷
留下明顯疤痕的記憶
閃電對妳是
點燃生命的火花
愛也來得突然
即使是一場
不可預料的暴風雨
沛然而下的雨量
可使萬物
得到照護滋養
心靈也在
震顫中更加靠近
享受到
暴風雨後
詩的安慰寧靜

冬季

在台灣
即使寒冬
難得會下雪
我在瑞士初履雪地
聽到雪花的聲音
都講德語
在白茫茫雪地上
枯枝開始抽芽
小草花掙扎出
一點點顏色
更鮮豔的是
沿著山坡向下
蜿蜒曲折滑動的
年輕色彩
生命在雪花飄拂下
昂揚
在冬季裡
室內有暖氣
壁爐暖和身體

心只有靠愛溫暖
我向妳伸出手
傳遞心意
在台灣少有寒冬
看到妳屋頂
庭院草木
滿布雪的場景
我想把台灣陽光
送給妳
太陽愛萬物
讓妳的花早開
讓妳的樹早青翠
讓妳的湖早融化
讓天鵝早回來
與妳作伴
我瞭解妳的心情
妳想講的話
變成一首一首的詩
不斷傳來、傳來、傳來

自由鳥

我天生是
一隻自由鳥
歌唱四季
在我棲息的
玉蘭花樹枝上
在我終生不離不棄的
台灣美麗島
歌唱獨立
面臨囚禁的威脅
我的朋友被關入監獄裡
成為殖民威權的俘虜
還有許多朋友
是在監獄外
不能隨意言語的
社會俘虜
我想告訴妳
許多台灣人都患過
失語症

我在詩裡挖掘

鳥語的鄉音

用花香

記錄島上的美麗與哀愁

連結成詩

找到世界窗口

那是廣大的空間

可以自由飛翔

開始歌唱愛

是的，我擁有兩個心靈

以兩條和諧的琴弦

拉出同一旋律

在妳的俘虜營

可自由諦聽鳥語

我自願成為妳的俘虜

形式

把我放在
妳的口袋裡時
我應該呈現
什麼樣的形式
一串鑰匙
一枚銅幣
還是妳的手機
打開時
就可聽到我聲音
看到我影像
或僅僅是
一張備忘錄
寫三個字
勿忘我

捉迷藏

不知道妳是我的影子

或我才是妳的影子

兩人離開遠遠

心卻重疊在一起

透過詩

成為我們的太陽

給我們溫暖

在陽光照耀下

妳影中有我

我影中有妳

不用躲藏

不用尋找

即使妳離開遠去

影子分離

詩路

詩路
是一條新路
從妳到我
的交通
沿路
有百靈鳥在唱
空中
有燕子在飛
林間
有蘭花在開
多麼奇異的是
看到無花果
不需經過開花階段
直接結果在
樹幹上
那是詩呀
路上
我發現
愛

如果我是雲

如果我是雲
每天早上叫醒妳
要鳥為妳唱歌
要風為妳吹笛
在窗外欣賞妳寫詩
傾聽妳朗誦
太陽出來把我照成
和妳一樣金髮
晚上為妳守門戶
讓妳睡得安隱
連夢都不會受打攪

今晚到妳夢裡來

今晚
我要搭弦月船
循銀河
到妳夢裡來
有黃昏星
為我餞行
月光陪伴我
以對妳的思念
做指南針
以對妳的渴望
做動力
今晚我要到妳夢裡來
準備帶給妳
台灣的熱情陽光
溫暖妳
雪天的心
把亞熱帶的熱情
照耀妳

思念中的場景
今晚我要到妳夢裡來
把詩親手獻給妳
朗讀給妳欣賞
以奧費斯的琴弦
演奏音樂
令人神往的天籟
我要沿銀河
摘取清香月桂花
編成花冠
請啟明星見證
戴在妳頭上
我一定
要到妳夢裡來
今晚

覆薩福

我無門可關
我是空間
妳是甜美的空氣
充滿我的整個宇宙
我的愛融入妳的空氣裡
拼合成整體氛圍
甜美、清新
譜成情歌交響樂

郵票

你是信件
把要說的話
折疊
密封在信封裡
我是郵票
貼在妳胸前
表示已經佔有
妳最貼心的位置
信封只是薄薄的分際
在那小小的空間
妳在裡面受到委曲
不能公開呼吸
我在外面自由自在
最瞭解妳的心意
堅守妳的祕密
我們同在
可以一起旅行
也可以一直躲在郵筒裡

當做遺失郵件
或許經過多少年後
偶然被發現
成為軼事或奇蹟
可能有人會多事做研究
信件只是一首詩
說不定字跡已然模糊
郵票已經褪色
不知道要寄去哪裡

實踐者

愛
有時像地震
無法預測何時發生
發生在哪一地點
有時像颱風
無法控制強度
引導往哪個方向
愛
有時無緣無故遇上
無法事先設計
要發生幾級地震
或是幾級颱風
情人呀
我們不是地震儀
也不可能是測候所
我們無法預言
不是先知
一旦事件來臨

我全心全意接受

愛

長相左右

距離不一定
是隔離
有詩相繫
瞬間天涯就在隔壁
詩的精靈
還可鑽入深心裡
把苦悶化成莫大喜悅
一如長相左右
毫無距離

越過海峽

愛情有時
是冒險的事業
像蝴蝶要飛越過海峽
尋找甜蜜的新生地
像群雁南飛時
堅持飛往北方的孤雁
很難預料
有什麼風暴即將來臨
也許是在創造歷史
也許只留下記憶
就像詩創作
一樣冒險
要踏過多少前人的足跡
要越過多少無人的叢林
也許攀登高峰
也許陷入沼澤
等待愛救援

還有一首詩

最後的詩之前

我還要寫一首詩

表示我的愛

我愛這個世界

雖然有些無人道的動亂

我愛祖國台灣

雖然一再被殖民

我愛喜歡我的朋友

雖然我不能令人滿意

我愛萬物

雖然我無能盡心保護

我愛詩

雖然不能安慰人人的心靈

我有寫不完的詩

要讓妳知道

我沒有盡到義務

所以在最後的詩之前

我還要寫一首詩

雖然常常無法預料
會寫成怎麼樣

沉默

即使沉默不語
我能瞭解妳的心意
因為妳已住在
我的心房裡
不會讓妳在門口等待
其實我已不設防
沒有門禁
沒有守衛
可以任妳進出
與我胸腔共同呼吸
妳的詩深深感動我
我也以詩回應
我能瞭解妳的心意
即使沉默不語

真愛

真愛
在一生裡
瞬間成為永恆
心心相繫
純潔可以比擬
白天鵝羽毛上水珠
在陽光下晶亮
薩福呀
聽妳心聲詠唱
還能要求
什麼是無悔的
真愛

妳知道

妳知道妳是誰
妳也知道
我明白妳是誰
在我內心
廣大的空間內
自由自在
妳可以像鳥築巢
像蜜蜂釀蜜
妳不必拘泥是薩福
妳是天使
可以在夢裡飛翔
在安詳的樂園

The Second String · 英語篇

李魁賢 著

Young Golden Bough

My young golden bough

I'm used to free

wandering everywhere

regardless at hillside or seashore.

Neither shadow nor trace when I come and go

I am fond of playing with trees

caressing their lush green hairs.

The blonde one is more attractive to me.

No matter when morning sunshine or evening glows

it displays the legend of golden bough

and seems to make me watching

the scenery either in previous life or afterlife world.

I am not indulged in dreaming

while the golden bough under the vast sky

forms a bridge leading to another world

connecting the open space on both sides

There is no door

so that no need to knock it

when I walked forward from this bank
you accept me on the opposite side.
My young golden bough
you are not necessary to wave your hand
or to emit any signal
I have seen you from afar
like the sunshine without any guidance
without obstructed by any shade.
As soon as I just lean down
there will be a reflection from you
like a rainbow bridge let me across
the flowing river.
I know that your bough
is longing for the kiss by my rays onto
your fine and gentle skin.
I love to hear the song of your whistle
singing the odes to four seasons.
Oh, you are my Sappho, my Muse!

I frequently incarnate myself as the wind
used to free wandering everywhere.
My young golden bough
no matter you are at hillside or seashore
anywhere you are
I will be around you
even if I have neither shadow nor trace.
You know, I'm in your heart!
You know, I'm in your heart!

Beloved

You asked me to write you
a letter about my love affairs.
In fact, many past events
have been lost in my memory.
With the change of time
some things are getting more and more blurred
while other things becoming clearer and clearer.
My brain now is just
a blank sheet of paper
and at this moment
only you
in my mind.
I tried to write down
all the names of the women that
I have connected,
it appears that all the names
are just the same as yours,
and it turned out to be you.

I am starting on the blank paper

to write the first page of love story

in which you are the heroine

to be always remembered,

and alive forever

in the world of love.

This time is yours,

This time is yours,

This time is yours.

Good Morning

Good morning!
It seems not so good to you.
After passing though the world of darkness
experienced with the darkness of the world
you have heard the people crying in the dark
have seen the people struggling at night.
Even when the new morning comes
you are still care about
the eagles preying the little birds in the sky
the tigers, leopards and lions hunting
reindeers and sheep on the steppe
while the other half of the earth
fallen into the condition without sunshine.
These really make you uneasy.
Yet, could you feel better if I beside you?

Poetry is Love

The God creates the love
spreading all over the universe.
The God also creates the poets
in praise of the love
for sunrise for sunset
for floral fragrances for bird chirps
for small grasses for big trees
for beasts for livestock
for the wind for the rain
for sad for joy
for meeting each other in laughing hugs
for parting to wave hands in tears.
In your poems
I feel the mutual attraction for loving poetry.
The images from natural things
express your passion your affection
because love is poetry
and poetry is love
is your calling.

Firefly

There are always fires in the life
lasting forever
naturally to raise the wind
transmitting Sappho's poems across the ocean.

It sounds beautiful tenderness
like an angel gospel,
I don't have to wait,
as soon as open my heart
it resonates in mind wholeheartedly.

The destiny of a poet
is the same as a firefly
just displaying
a faint light to the world
in the darkness of the wild.
Someone dislikes it too gloomy
while others get comfortable.

That dim light maybe
without warmth as a fireplace,
yet it is a hope of the soul
like a lighthouse at seaside
indicating the vessel
to beach safely.

Oh my Sappho,
when someday
you become a seagull
there are reefs for you to stay,
there are land for you to nest
for you to derive life here.

Sacred Love

Love is a sacred word

becoming a gospel

combining truth, goodness and beauty in one.

From the beginning of the World

love is the fundamental of everything.

People are born of love,

people also die of love.

Love is the driving force behind the world

always sacred

always warm.

The universe

is alive endlessly.

The Raven No Longer Fly

When I miss you
I will write poetry
rather than any letter.
I will send a pigeon to you
do not bother a raven.
I worry about his ominous tuxedo
would cause surprise
and scare you by knocking on the door.
I know you are not Lenore.
There is no war in the sky nowadays
the raven no longer fly,
my pigeon
will fly freely
bringing freedom message of Taiwan
to you at dawn.
I will always remember
you are blonde Elvira.

Storm

Sudden lightning
displays an alarm
an unpredictable storm to come.
The sky can be hurt
to leave a memory of marked scars.
To you lightning is
lighting a fire of being.
Love is coming suddenly
even if it is a
an unpredictable storm.
The amount of rainfall
will make everything
well cared and nourished.
The souls are also
getting closer in trembling
and enjoy
the silent comfort of poetry
after the storm.

The Winter

In Taiwan
even though during cold winter
it has hardly snow.
When I was on the snow land in Switzerland
I heard the sound of snowflakes
in speaking German language.
From the white snow land
the dry branches start to sprout
the grass flowers emerge
a few colors,
yet more colorful is
the vivid young figures
sliding zigzag down
along the hillside slope.
Lives under the ethereal snowflakes
are energetic.
In winter
there is heating indoor,
the fireplace warms the body

only love can warm the heart.
I reach out my hand to you
transmitting my best regards.
With rare cold winter in Taiwan
I find the roof of your house
even plants and grasses in your garden
covered with snow all over,
I wish to deliver the sunlight from Taiwan
for you.
The sun loves everything
would make your flowers bloom earlier
your trees green earlier
the lake melt earlier
let the swan come back earlier
as your companion.
I understand your feeling
what you want to say
becomes one after another poem
constantly send me, send me, send me.

Free Bird

I was born

a free bird

in praise of four seasons

among the Magnolia branches

of my habitat.

On Taiwan, Formosa island

my eternal homeland,

in praise of independence

I faced with the threat of imprisonment.

My friends were jailed

becoming the prisoners under colonial power,

there are many other friends

outside the jail

as prisoners in a society

no free speech allowable.

I want to tell you

many Taiwanese have been suffered

from aphasia.

I searched in poetry

the mother tongue of birds,

to connect poems

with fragrance of flowers

in recording the beauty and mourning on the island,

and found a window towards outside world

that is a vast space

available for flying freely

at the beginning in praise of love.

Yes, I have two souls

to play two harmonious strings

in one and the same melody.

In the captive camp of your love

I am free listening to the languages of birds

willing to become your prisoner.

Form

When you carry me

in your pocket

What kind of form

should I present?

A bunch of keys,

a copper coin,

or your mobile phone

as soon as opening

you can hear my voice,

see my video,

or just

a piece of memo

with three words

Forget Me Not.

Hide and Seek

Whether you are my shadow
or instead I am your shadow,
we two are even far away
yet our hearts are overlapped together.
Through poetry
which becomes our sun
gives us warm,
under the sunshine
there is me in your shadow
and you in mine,
neither to hide
nor to look for.
Even if you go away
our shadows separate
our hearts still overlap together.

Poetry Road

Poetry Road
is a new way
in communication
from you to me.
Along the road
there are larks singing.
In the air
there are swallows flying.
Among the trees
there are orchids blooming.
What strange enough is
the fig I found
their fruits are bore
on the trunk
without the flowering stage.
That is the poetry!
I find
on the road
Love.

If I am a Cloud

If I am a cloud
every morning to wake you up
to ask the bird singing for you
to please the wind playing flute for you
through window to appreciate you writing poetry
to listen your recital.
When the sun emerges to radiate me
as a blonde just like you.
At night I will stay at your home as a guard
keeping you a sound sleep
even undisturbed in dream.

Visit You in Dream Tonight

Tonight

I want to board on a crescent boat

sailing along the Milky Way

to visit you in dream.

There is Hesperus evening star

saying bon voyage to me,

and moonlight in accompany with me.

There is missing to you

as my compass,

and longing for you

as my generator.

I'm going to visit you in dream tonight.

I'm preparing to bring you

warm sunshine from Taiwan

to warm up your heart

in snowy weather,

let subtropical passion

illuminate you

in the memorial scenery.

I'm going to visit you in dream tonight.

I will dedicate my poetry to you

read it to win your appreciation

with Orpheus's lyre strings

playing the music

as celestial sound.

I want to navigate along the Milky Way

picking fragrant laurel flowers

woven into a wreath

to crown you

under the witness of Venus morning star.

I'm certainly

going to visit you in dream

tonight.

To Sappho

I have no door to close
I am a free space
You are the sweet air
fulfilled my entire universe
My love solvated into your air
merged as a whole atmosphere
sweet, fresh and
composed into a symphonic love song

The Stamp

You are a letter

all you want to say

folded

and sealed within an envelope.

I am a stamp

posted in front of your chest

it represents to have possessed a position

closest to your heart.

The envelope is only a negligible separation

and within that small space

you wronged inside

can't breathe publicly.

I feel free and comfortable outside

best for understanding your mind,

and able to keep firmly your secret.

We are always together

either as travel companion

or staying in the mailbox all the way

being treated as a lost mail.
Maybe after many years
occasionally discovered
becoming an anecdote or a miracle.
Some busybodies may do research
why the letter is just simply one poem
and maybe the writing has already blurred
even the stamps have faded
nowhere to send.

Practitioner

Love

sometimes like an earthquake

unable to predict when it will happen

where did it happen,

sometimes like a typhoon

unable to control its intensity

which direction to guide.

Love

sometimes encounters occasionally

unable to design in advance

what magnitude of earthquake to occur

what scale of typhoon to reach.

Oh darling

we are neither a seismograph

nor a weather station.

We cannot predict

not a prophet.

Once the event comes

I accept wholeheartedly

Love.

Always together

The distance is not necessarily
caused separation.
So long as poetry connection existed
even remote distance is just like at next door.
The spirit of poetry
can penetrate into deep heart
turning the agony into joyful
so as always together
without any distance.

Cross the Strait

Love sometimes

is a venture business,

like a butterfly to fly over the strait

looking for a sweet new land

like one goose keeps its flight to the north lonely

when a flock of geese flying southward.

It is difficult to predict

what storm will be coming soon,

maybe creating a new history

maybe only leaving some memories behind.

Love is as venturous as

poetry creation,

to step over many footprints left by predecessors

to pass through many untrodden forests

maybe climbing up to the peak

maybe sunk into the swamp

waiting for love to rescue.

One More Poem

Before the last poem

I have still one more poem to write

in expression of my love.

I love this world

although there are some inhuman turmoil.

I love my motherland Taiwan

although it has been repeatedly colonized.

I love my friends who fond of me

although I am not quite satisfied.

I love everything

although I am unable to protect them wholeheartedly.

I love poetry

although I cannot comfort the souls of everyone.

I have numberless poems to write

let you know

I have not fulfilled my obligations.

Before the last poem

I have still one more poem to write

although often unpredictable

how will it be written

Silence

Even in silence
I can understand your feeling
because you have lived
within the room of my heart.
I will not let you wait at the door,
in fact, I have no defense
no access control
no guard to protect.
You can go in and out as you like
breathing together on my chest.
Your poems touch me so deeply
I respond you with poetry too.
I can understand your feeling
even in silence.

Authentic Love

Authentic love,

in one's lifetime,

makes a moment becoming an eternity.

Tying soul to soul

its purity is comparable as

the water pearl drops on the white swan feathers

shining under the sunshine.

O Sappho

When I listen to the melody of your poetry

who can ask for

what un-regretted

authentic love.

You Know

You do know who you are
you also know
that I understand who you are.
Within the vast space
of my heart
you may freely
to build a nest like a bird
to make honey like a honeybee.
You don't have to be Sappho
you are rather an angel
able flying in the dream
over the peaceful paradise.

Contents

語言文學類　PG2224　名流詩叢33

兩弦 Two Strings
——漢英雙語詩集

作　　　者/艾薇拉·辜柔維琪（Elvira Kujovic）、李魁賢（Lee Kuei-shien）
譯　　　者/李魁賢（Lee Kuei-shien）
責任編輯/林昕平
圖文排版/林宛榆
封面設計/蔡瑋筠

發　行　人/宋政坤
法律顧問/毛國樑　律師
出版發行/秀威資訊科技股份有限公司
　　　　　114台北市內湖區瑞光路76巷65號1樓
　　　　　電話：+886-2-2796-3638　傳真：+886-2-2796-1377
　　　　　http://www.showwe.com.tw
劃撥帳號/19563868　戶名：秀威資訊科技股份有限公司
　　　　　讀者服務信箱：service@showwe.com.tw
展售門市/國家書店（松江門市）
　　　　　104台北市中山區松江路209號1樓
　　　　　電話：+886-2-2518-0207　傳真：+886-2-2518-0778
網路訂購/秀威網路書店：https://store.showwe.tw
　　　　　國家網路書店：https://www.govbooks.com.tw

2019年8月　BOD一版
定價：220元
版權所有　翻印必究
本書如有缺頁、破損或裝訂錯誤，請寄回更換

國家圖書館出版品預行編目

兩弦：漢英雙語詩集 / 艾薇拉.辜柔維琪(Elvira
Kujovic), 李魁賢合著, 李魁賢譯. -- 一版. --
臺北市：秀威資訊科技, 2019.08
　面；　公分. -- (語言文學類)(名流詩叢；33)
BOD版
譯自：Two strings
ISBN 978-986-326-713-3(平裝)

813.1　　　　　　　　　　　　　　　108011055

讀者回函卡

感謝您購買本書，為提升服務品質，請填妥以下資料，將讀者回函卡直接寄回或傳真本公司，收到您的寶貴意見後，我們會收藏記錄及檢討，謝謝！如您需要了解本公司最新出版書目、購書優惠或企劃活動，歡迎您上網查詢或下載相關資料：http:// www.showwe.com.tw

您購買的書名：＿＿＿＿＿＿＿＿＿＿＿＿＿＿＿＿＿＿＿＿＿＿＿＿

出生日期：＿＿＿＿年＿＿＿＿月＿＿＿＿日

學歷：□高中 (含) 以下　　□大專　　□研究所 (含) 以上

職業：□製造業　□金融業　□資訊業　□軍警　□傳播業　□自由業
　　　□服務業　□公務員　□教職　　□學生　□家管　　□其它＿＿＿

購書地點：□網路書店　□實體書店　□書展　□郵購　□贈閱　□其他

您從何得知本書的消息？

　□網路書店　□實體書店　□網路搜尋　□電子報　□書訊　□雜誌
　□傳播媒體　□親友推薦　□網站推薦　□部落格　□其他＿＿＿＿＿

您對本書的評價：（請填代號　1.非常滿意　2.滿意　3.尚可　4.再改進）

　封面設計＿＿＿　版面編排＿＿＿　內容＿＿＿　文／譯筆＿＿＿　價格＿＿＿

讀完書後您覺得：

　□很有收穫　□有收穫　□收穫不多　□沒收穫

對我們的建議：＿＿＿＿＿＿＿＿＿＿＿＿＿＿＿＿＿＿＿＿＿＿

＿＿＿＿＿＿＿＿＿＿＿＿＿＿＿＿＿＿＿＿＿＿＿＿＿＿＿＿＿＿

＿＿＿＿＿＿＿＿＿＿＿＿＿＿＿＿＿＿＿＿＿＿＿＿＿＿＿＿＿＿

＿＿＿＿＿＿＿＿＿＿＿＿＿＿＿＿＿＿＿＿＿＿＿＿＿＿＿＿＿＿

11466
台北市內湖區瑞光路 76 巷 65 號 1 樓

秀威資訊科技股份有限公司　　　收

BOD 數位出版事業部

⋯⋯⋯⋯⋯⋯⋯⋯⋯⋯⋯⋯⋯⋯⋯⋯⋯⋯⋯⋯⋯⋯⋯⋯⋯⋯

（請沿線對折寄回，謝謝！）

姓　　名：＿＿＿＿＿＿＿＿　年齡：＿＿＿＿　性別：□女　□男

郵遞區號：□□□□□

地　　址：＿＿＿＿＿＿＿＿＿＿＿＿＿＿＿＿＿＿＿＿＿＿＿＿

聯絡電話：(日) ＿＿＿＿＿＿＿＿＿＿＿　(夜) ＿＿＿＿＿＿＿＿＿＿

E-mail：＿＿＿＿＿＿＿＿＿＿＿＿＿＿＿＿＿＿＿＿＿＿＿＿